Weirdo Zoo

Catherine Johnson

TO K.E.Y.S
Stay weird!
Best wishes,
Catherine
CSd

ISBN:-13:978-1491019320
ISBN-10:1491019328

Dedication

For Sharon.

CONTENTS

Has Zebra left the zoo?

Giraffe woke up and looked around, where was her stripy friend?

"He must be hiding somewhere near, I must check round the bend."

Giraffe appeared at Camel house,   where Camels munched on hay.

"Hey you! Has Zebra left the zoo?"

"We're busy go away!"

Giraffe found Penguins playing out, they scuttled off to swim.

"Hey you! Has Zebra left the zoo?"

"I think the mouse saw him."

She heard a squeak from down below, bent down and saw the mouse.

"Little Mouse have you seen Zebra?"

"Well no, he's in his house."

Arriving to a busy scene, Giraffe shooed off the sheep.

"I've searched around the zoo for you, and you were in your keep."

"Oh daft Giraffe, I fell asleep. I've been at home all day.

I can't believe you dashed around, while I slept on some hay."

King Rhino and Queen Hippo

Black caped rhino

Hippo in a tutu

Feathers and thunder

Twirl, charge, crash!

Little Monkey

One day last week I nearly sold you to the local zoo,

Your antics led me to believe you were a kangaroo.

Today I see you differently, you're acting kind of funky,

But we're still going to the zoo cause you're a little monkey.

Never go picnicking with Elephants loose

Mrs. Peabody arrived at the zoo

with a hat and a smile and a picnic for two.

She laid down her blanket, a nice gingham red,

"What a beautiful day for a picnic," she said.

She picked up a sandwich of lettuce and ham,

while hubby preferred to eat pickles and spam.

They munched on some carrots and sipped cranberry juice.

Little did they know there's elephants loose.

If only they'd sat just a few feet away

Their beautiful picnic might've lasted the day.

Mr. Peabody glanced up at the sky,

Thinking that thunder was sure to pass by.

Little did he know, that wasn't the case.

No thunder today just an elephant race.

The warnings went out but neither could hear,

Their hearing aids needing a tweak twice a year.

The elephants brrrrd a huge elephant sound,

In shock they dropped all of their food on the ground.

Now up on their knees, arthritic and slow,

A teeny bit faster they needed to go.

Oops they're too late, here comes the stampede.

Knocked over, surprised, the poor dears weed.

Squish went the sandwiches, spilled went the juice.

Never go picnicking with elephants loose.

Boring Birds

No one writes about the birds in cages at the zoo,

Boring, snoring, preening plumage

What else do we do?

But let me tell you right away,

This gets me all a flutter

We are a lovely flock of birds

Except Borris, he's a nutter.

Frogoloctopus

One day a frog fell off its log, sunk to the riverbed.

There it saw an Octopus and this is what it said,

"Are you a Frogoloctopus?"

The frog croaked back, "Not I."

But then he saw his tentacles and had a little cry.

The Otter One

An otter and a beaver got confused

They forgot which was which.

"I'm the otter."

"No, I'm the otter."

There was only one way to settle the matter.

"You be the otter. And I'll be the otter one."

Zulu Beaver

River warrior

Uses teeth to sharpen spear

Lunch is to the point.

Kirk's Dik Dik

Zig zag
Game of tag
Nose to nose
Big bright clothes
Furry crest
The best dressed nest
Lurky kirky
Dik dik.

Hip Hip Hooray!

Today's the parade, hip hip hooray!

Lot's of dancing all the day.

Heaps of fun from snakes to bats,

hippos too and Meer cats.

Tigers, donkeys, wild boar pigs,

Emus dancing wearing wigs.

Hip hip hooray Giraffe's amused,

but Zebra's hiding, he's confused.

Aardwolf

I smell you little termites
I slink, and wink and scowl.
My name is Ardy Aardwolf
I'm Aardvaark plus a howl.
Aaaoooooh!

Goat Afloat

A talking goat
A giddy goat
A silly goat
A billy goat
A silly coat
A talking moat
A giddy boat
A goat afloat.

Bobcat
Does a Bobcat bob?
Does it even meow?
Does it fetch and carry dirt?
Tell me how. Tell me how.

Richard and Isabelle

Richard the Flamingo does one-legged whirls,

Isabelle the Ostrich, all feathers and twirls.

He's beaky and geeky,

She's peaky and cheeky.

What a great show for the boys and the girls.

Hee Haw!

A pair of miniature donkeys,

the latest addition to the zoo,

caught the eye of Orangutang

and also cheeky Roo.

Orangutan was crazy,

he rode his donkey too hard.

Roo had trouble holding on

and Kangarolled right down the yard.

Southern Elephant Seal

Two enormous elephant seals
Compete to see who is the biggest.
They are still weighing in on the results.

Guinea! Guinea!

Here guinea, guinea, little guinea pig,
Let's all wiggle to the guinea pig jig.
    Shuffle to the water,
    Shuffle to the pellets,
    Shuffle with my brothers
    And the neighboring ferrets.

Here guinea, guinea, little guinea pig,
Let's all wiggle to the guinea pig jig.
    Twitch to the left,
    Twitch to the right,
    Twitch in the morning,
    Twitch in the night.

Here guinea, guinea, little guinea pig,
Let's all wiggle to the guinea pig jig.
    Shimmy in circles,
    Shimmy in rows,
    Shimmy with your zoo friends
    On knees and elbows.

Here guinea, guinea, little guinea pig,
It's the end of your silly billy, guinea, jiggle jig.

Frankenguin

I wibble and I wobble my long bat wings
I stick and I stake my fangs into things.
I swim and I fly but not both together,
Except around midnight, depends on the weather.

Sophie's Suds

Sophie the hippo was due for a bath, but clumsy Richard boy was he daft.

Poured too many bubbles, his hand went and slipped.

With problems like these he was most ill-equipped.

Sophie was there with her shower cap and brush,

Scratching her back she had no need to rush.

But the bubbles grew higher spilling over the side

And away flew Sophie to the countryside.

Wordy Wildebeest

A herd of wordy wildebeest
Wrote poems by the fence.
They used their teeth to hold their pens
Not many words made sense.

The Okapi stood listening
As the wildebeest recited
Their poems about adventures
Now the listeners grew excited.

The lions heard a whisper
Of these poems and replied,
"You write so foul, we're on the prowl
You'd better stay inside."

The poetry kept flowing out,
So angry lions encroached
Upon the pen of wildebeest
Notepads, and pens were poached.

The lions pinned a notice up,
"No poetry recitals.
Let it be said, you have been warned
Or we'll be back for vitals."

Drifting Dromedary

One day a dromedary drifted by
Decidedly upside down
'Cause in the desert dry as toast
A sandstorm rode through town.

Stork's Walk

There once was a rather tall stork

So tall he could hardly walk

We bought him some shoes

That looked like canoes

Now he water-skis pulled by a hawk.

Giraffes in a knot

Giraffes in a knot.

All reaching for the same branch

Knot a good idea.

Okapi

Whatever is an Okapi?
That pees to mark its territory.
It's legs look like a Zebra's
It's tongue as long as Giraffe's
I think the zoo got all mixed up
It's big ears heard me. Quick! Run!

Turkey Vultures

What a pair of turkey vultures

Walking down the path.

Stinky, smelly, turkey vultures

Both in need of a bath.

One had on a pair of socks

Stripey, bright and wrinkled.

The other wore a pom pom hat

And frequently stopped and tinkled.

The turkey in socks is called Froob.

The one with the pom pom is Bean.

Froob was loud, he'd dance in the street,

But Bean preferred not to be seen.

Greater Rhia

There once was a bird called a Rhea
Who got something stuck in his ee-yuh
And he did scream and shout
Until the day it crawled out
And said, 'No need to shout, I'm right ee-yuh.'

Pigeon Bop

Fidgety, pigeoty,
Scritch, scratch,
Hop.
Fidgety, pigeoty
To the pigeon bop.

Crocodiles don't eat soup

Munchy, crunchy.

Chompy, chewy.

Eat it quick, no runny stewy.

No more slop, no more gloop,

'Cause crocodiles don't eat soup.

Super Tall Giraffe

I hear scrambling over there
I hear shuffling by my feet,
I hear shouting from behind
'cause I've shot up fifty feet.

Orangutan

Orang U
Orang U
Orangutan
Where were you?
Orang U
Orang U
Orangutan
To tell you to meet me at the zoo.

I howl
Never scowl
Or prowl
Nor am I fowl
What am I?

(Howler Monkey)

Tawny Owl

Tawny Yawny
Scrawny owl
Hooty, scooty,
Screechy owl
Eeky, meeky,
Seeky owl.
Yawny, yarny,
Barny owl.

Weirdo Zoo

Giraffes aren't yellow they are blue

only here at Weirdo zoo.

Flamingoes hop around and wink,

Hippos try to swim but sink.

Tigers dance and zebras fly,

high up in the turquoise sky.

Magic dolphins disappear,

invisible for half the year.

Elephants stomp and paint the ground,

the brightest footprints all around.

Zoo keepers carry umbrellas,

they sure are peculiar fellas.

Would you like to join us too?

There's always room at Weirdo Zoo.

ABOUT THE AUTHOR

Catherine Johnson is a British Ex-Pat living in Canada with her delightful family. Has Zebra Left the Zoo? Never Go Picnicking With Elephants Loose and Wordy Wildebeest have been previously published by the Poetry Institute of Canada. You can read more of Catherine's poetry on her blog: http://catherinemjohnson.wordpress.com

Many thanks to my blog readers, 12x12 group, WANA friends and poetry wisdom from Jeanne Poland and Freeda Baker-Nichols. Thanks also to my patient family. You are all awesome!

Twitter: @CatherinePoet
Facebook: www.facebook.com/catherine.m.johnson

Keep an eye out for weirdos at the zoo!

Made in the USA
Charleston, SC
06 March 2014